GENERAL STORE

by **Rachel Field**
illustrated by **Giles Laroche**

SCHOLASTIC INC.
New York Toronto London Auckland Sydney

Also illustrated by Giles Laroche
Sing a Song of People

ISBN 0-590-43687-2
Text for "General Store" is from the book *Taxis and
Toadstools* by Rachel Field. Copyright © 1926 by
Rachel Field; renewed 1953 by Arthur S. Pederson.
Reprinted by permission of Doubleday and Company.
Illustrations copyright © 1988 by Giles Laroche.
All rights reserved. Published by Scholastic Inc.,
730 Broadway, New York, NY 10003, by arrangement with
Little, Brown and Company, Inc.

12 11 10 9 8 7 6 5 4 3   4 5/9

Printed in the U.S.A.   23
First Scholastic printing, October 1990

To Claire and Romeo

— G.L.

Someday I'm going to have a store
With a tinkly bell hung over the door,

With real glass cases and counters wide

And drawers all spilly with things inside.

There'll be a little of everything:

Bolts of calico;

balls of string;

Jars of peppermint;

tins of tea;

Pots and kettles and crockery;

Seeds in packets;

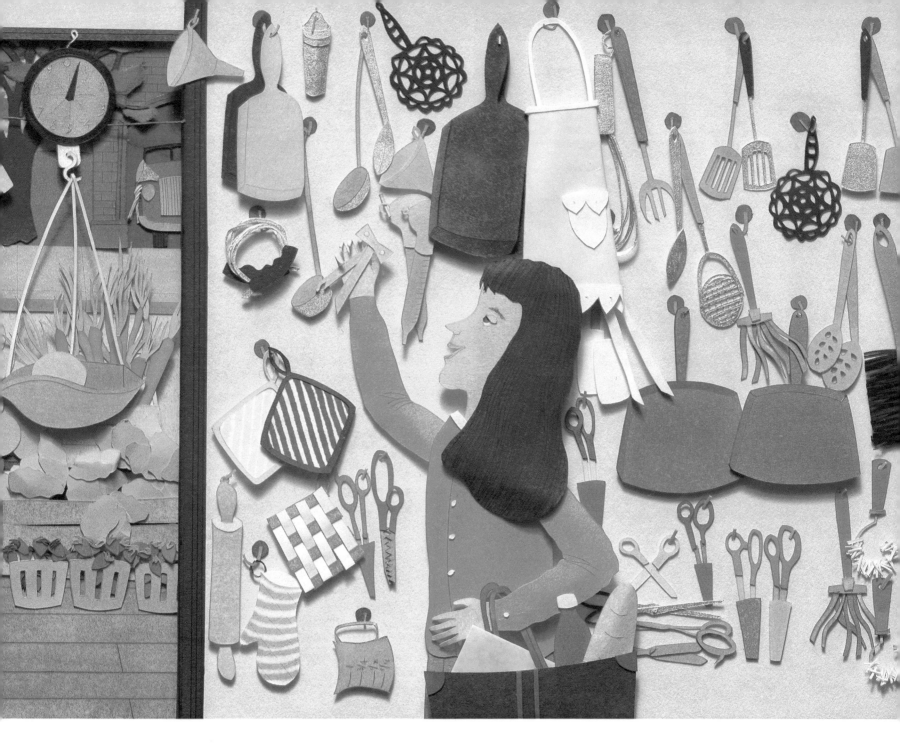

scissors bright;

Kegs of sugar, brown and white;

Sarsaparilla for picnic lunches,

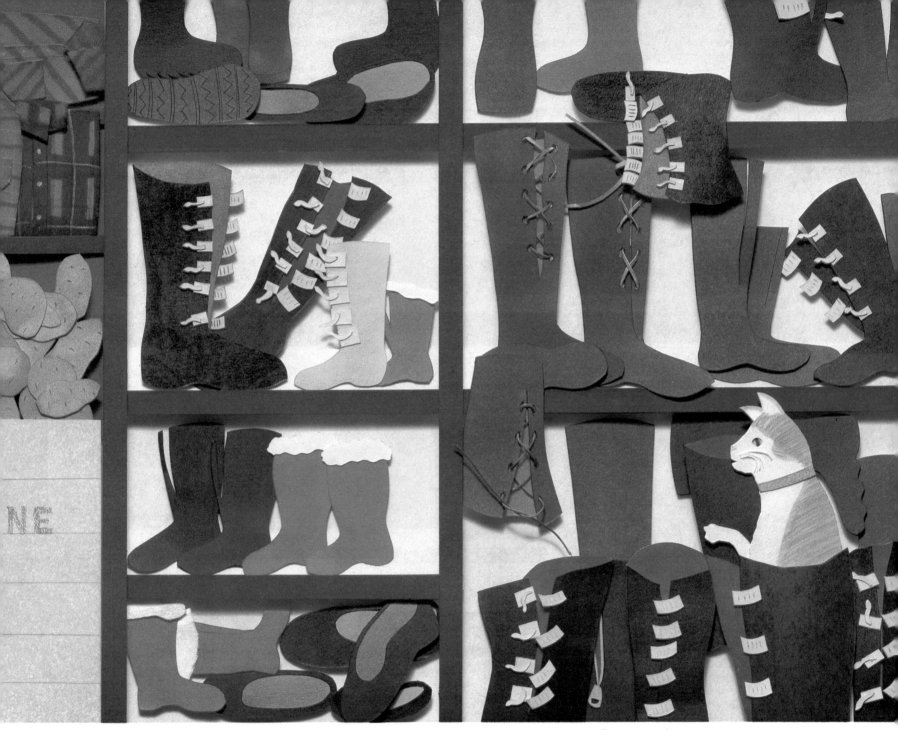

Bananas and rubber boots in bunches.

I'll fix the window and dust each shelf,

And take the money in all myself,

It will be my store and I will say:
"What can I do for you to-day?"